MR. FORGETFUL

by Roger Hargreaves

It was one of those beautiful summer mornings that everybody likes to see.

In Forget-me-not Cottage the owner was fast asleep.

Mr Forgetful.

He was having a dream.

Then the sun streaming through the windows woke up Mr Forgetful.

"Ohhhh," he yawned, and stretched his arms, and tried to remember what he had been dreaming about.

But of course he couldn't, because Mr Forgetful can't remember anything.

Anything at all!

Ever!

Mr Forgetful got out of bed and went to wash his face.

But he'd forgotten where the bathroom was in his house, and do you know what he did?

He walked into the wardrobe!

"Silly me," he giggled to himself.

Eventually, of course, Mr Forgetful found his bathroom and washed his face.

He even remembered to clean his teeth!

Then he went downstairs to make himself some breakfast.

He toasted some bread. But of course he forgot about it and it was burnt.

He boiled himself an egg. But of course he forgot about it and it was hard boiled.

Mr Forgetful has burnt toast and hard boiled eggs for breakfast every day!

It was such a lovely day Mr Forgetful decided to walk down to the village to buy a stamp for a letter he'd written three weeks ago but had forgotten to post.

Off he set.

And did he remember to shut the door of Forget-me-not Cottage behind him?

Of course he didn't!

"Good morning, Mr Forgetful," said Mrs Parcel in the village post office. "What can I do for you this fine morning?"

"I'd like a . . . er . . . a . . . er . . . um . . . I've forgotten," he said.

"A stamp?" suggested Mrs Parcel looking at the letter Mr Forgetful was carrying.

"Yes! A stamp! That's what it was I was trying to remember not to forget," said Mr Forgetful.

Mrs Parcel smiled. She was used to Mr Forgetful.

Mr Forgetful had some more shopping to do.

But could he remember what it was he was supposed to remember not to forget to shop for?

Of course he couldn't!

So, he decided to go home.

On his way he met the village policeman going the other way.

"Morning, Mr Forgetful," said the policeman. "Will you give Farmer Fields a message from me on your way home please?"

Farmer Fields had a farm not very far from Forget-me-not Cottage.

"Tell him there's a sheep loose in the lane!" said the policeman.

Poor Mr Forgetful.

He'd never had a message to remember in his life before.

"There's a sheep loose in the lane," he said to himself trying to remember the message as he hurried along. "There's a sheep loose in the lane. There's a sheep loose in the lane."

"There's a sheep loose in the lane!"

"There's a sheep loose in the lane!"

Mr Forgetful repeated the message over and over to himself.

"There's a sheep loose in the lane!"

Eventually he arrived at the farm and found Farmer Fields.

"Mr Fields," he said, "there's a goose asleep in the rain!"

Farmer Fields couldn't believe his ears.

"There's a goose asleep in the rain?" repeated Farmer Fields slowly. "But I don't have any geese, and anyway it isn't raining. Are you sure that was the message?"

Poor Mr Forgetful. He'd got it all wrong, and he couldn't remember how to get it all right.

He simply couldn't remember at all.

So, off he went home. Poor Mr Forgetful.

Mr Forgetful walked away from Farmer Field's farm feeling very sorry for himself.

"I wish I could remember things," he thought.

He was so busy feeling sorry for himself that he didn't see that there was a sheep loose in the lane.

He bumped into it and fell over.

"Bother," said Mr Forgetful.

"Baa," said the sheep.

"How silly letting a sheep loose in the lane," thought Mr Forgetful.

And then, he remembered the message.

He jumped up and ran back along the lane to the farm as fast as he could.

"Mr Fields! Mr Fields!" he called as he ran into the farmyard. "Mr Fields! There's a . . . there's a goose asleep in the rain!"

He'd forgotten again!

Mr Fields scratched his head.

"Come with me. Come on," cried Mr Forgetful, and pulled Farmer Fields back along the lane until they came to the sheep that was loose.

"There it is," cried Mr Forgetful, pointing.
"A goose!"

And then he stopped. "Oh dear," he said. "That's not a goose, is it? That's a sheep!" And he blushed.

"I think," smiled Farmer Fields, "that you're the goose!"

And he chuckled.

And Mr Forgetful giggled.

And Farmer Fields laughed.

And even the sheep started to laugh it was so funny.

Later that day, Mr Forgetful sat down in his favourite armchair in Forget-me-not Cottage to think about what a funny day it had been.

But do you know something?

He tried and tried, but try as he would he simply couldn't remember anything that had happened.

Oh, Mr Forgetful!

3 Great Offers for **MR. MEN** Fans!

MR. MEN TOKEN

1 New Mr. Men or Little Miss Library Bus Presentation Cases

A brand new stronger, roomier school bus library box, with sturdy carrying handle and stay-closed fasteners.
The full colour, wipe-clean boxes make a great home for your full collection.
They're just £5.99 inc P&P and free bookmark!

☐ MR. MEN   ☐ LITTLE MISS (please tick and order overleaf)

2 Door Hangers and Posters

In every Mr. Men and Little Miss book like this one, you will find a special token. Collect 6 tokens and we will send you a brilliant Mr. Men or Little Miss poster and a Mr. Men or Little Miss double sided full colour bedroom door hanger of your choice. Simply tick your choice in the list and tape a 50p coin for your two items to this page.

PLEASE STICK YOUR 50P COIN HERE

Door Hangers (please tick)
☐ Mr. Nosey & Mr. Muddle
☐ Mr. Slow & Mr. Busy
☐ Mr. Messy & Mr. Quiet
☐ Mr. Perfect & Mr. Forgetful
☐ Little Miss Fun & Little Miss Late
☐ Little Miss Helpful & Little Miss Tidy
☐ Little Miss Busy & Little Miss Brainy
☐ Little Miss Star & Little Miss Fun

Posters (please tick)
☐ MR.MEN
☐ LITTLE MISS

They're very special collector's items!
Simply tick your first and second* choices from the list below
of any 2 characters!

1st Choice

- ☐ Mr. Happy
- ☐ Mr. Lazy
- ☐ Mr. Topsy-Turvy
- ☐ Mr. Bounce
- ☐ Mr. Bump
- ☐ Mr. Small
- ☐ Mr. Snow
- ☐ Mr. Wrong

- ☐ Mr. Daydream
- ☐ Mr. Tickle
- ☐ Mr. Greedy
- ☐ Mr. Funny
- ☐ Little Miss Giggles
- ☐ Little Miss Splendid
- ☐ Little Miss Naughty
- ☐ Little Miss Sunshine

2nd Choice

- ☐ Mr. Happy
- ☐ Mr. Lazy
- ☐ Mr. Topsy-Turvy
- ☐ Mr. Bounce
- ☐ Mr. Bump
- ☐ Mr. Small
- ☐ Mr. Snow
- ☐ Mr. Wrong

- ☐ Mr. Daydream
- ☐ Mr. Tickle
- ☐ Mr. Greedy
- ☐ Mr. Funny
- ☐ Little Miss Giggles
- ☐ Little Miss Splendid
- ☐ Little Miss Naughty
- ☐ Little Miss Sunshine

*Only in case your first choice is out of stock.

─── **TO BE COMPLETED BY AN ADULT** ───

**To apply for any of these great offers, ask an adult to complete the coupon below and send it with
the appropriate payment and tokens, if needed, to MR. MEN CLASSIC OFFER, PO BOX 715, HORSHAM RH12 5WG**

☐ Please send ____ Mr. Men Library case(s) and/or ____ Little Miss Library case(s) at £5.99 each inc P&P

☐ Please send a poster and door hanger as selected overleaf. I enclose six tokens plus a 50p coin for P&P

☐ Please send me ____ pair(s) of Mr. Men/Little Miss fridge magnets, as selected above at £2.00 inc P&P

Fan's Name _____

Address _____

_____ **Postcode** _____

Date of Birth _____

Name of Parent/Guardian _____

Total amount enclosed £ _____

☐ I enclose a cheque/postal order payable to Egmont Books Limited

☐ **Please charge my MasterCard/Visa/Amex/Switch or Delta account** (delete as appropriate)

Card Number

Expiry date ___ / ___   **Signature** _____

MR.MEN   **LITTLE MISS**
Mr. Men and Little Miss™ & ©Mrs. Roger Hargreaves

CUT ALONG DOTTED LINE AND RETURN THIS WHOLE PAGE